THE MAGICAL, MYSTICAL, MARVELOUS COAT

by Catherine Ann Cullen

Illustrated by David Christiana

Little, Brown and Company
Boston New York London

First Edition

Library of Congress Cataloging-in-Publication Data

Cullen, Catherine Ann.
   The magical, mystical, marvelous coat / by Catherine Ann Cullen ; illustrated by David Christiana — 1st ed.
     p. cm.
   Summary: The unusual buttons from a young girl's favorite coat provide magical assistance to a giant, a swan, some sailors, a wizard, some rabbits, and an elf.
   ISBN 0-316-16334-1
   [1. Buttons — Fiction. 2. Magic — Fiction. 3. Stories in rhyme.]
I. Christiana, David, ill. II. Title.

PZ8.3.C8885 Mag 2001
[E] — dc21   00-034815

10 9 8 7 6 5 4 3 2 1

TWP

Printed in Singapore

The text was set in Garth Graphic and the title type is Miehle Classic Condensed.
The artwork for this book was done in watercolor on Arches 300-pound
hot press watercolor paper.

Stitched with love for the magical, mystical, marvelous coterie:
Olivia Fountain, Emma Fountain, and Tom Finnegan
Go maire sibh is go gcaithe sibh é!
(Long life to wear it, and may ye outlive it!)

C. A. C.

To Kathe and Wylie

D. C.

The coat that I wear from the fall to the spring

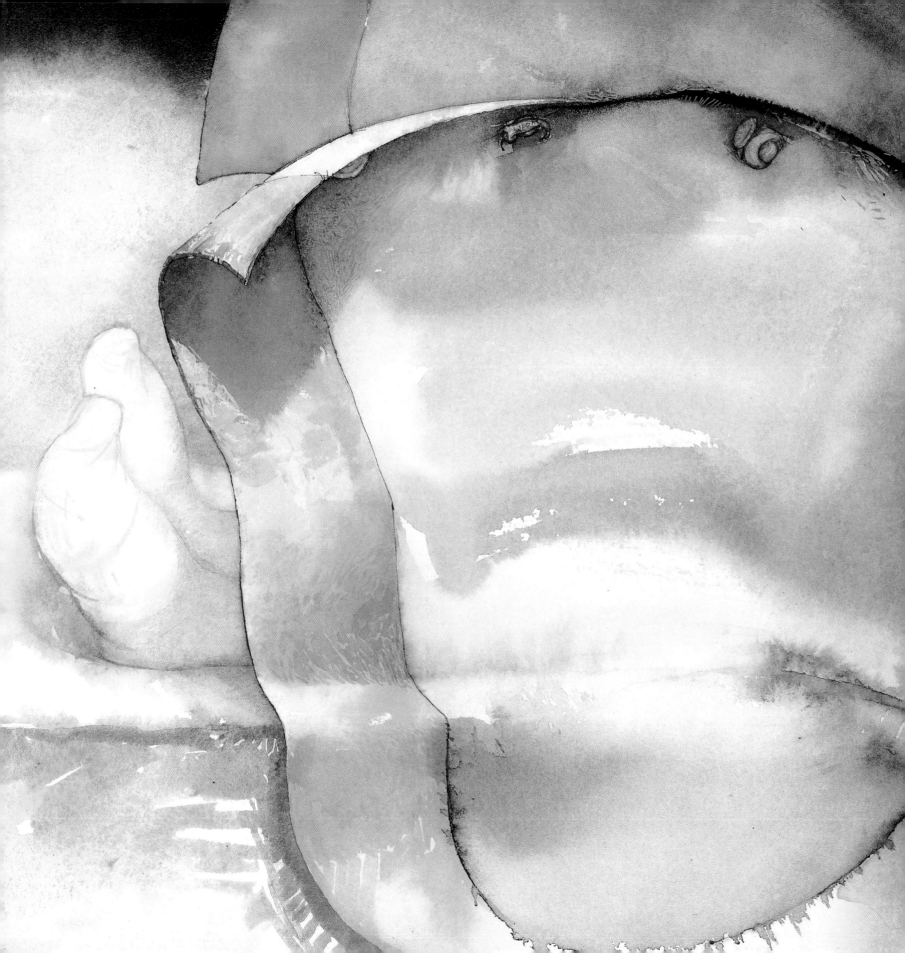

Is my chunkiest, funkiest, favorite thing.
But the six reasons why it's a magical coat

are the buttons that go from the heel
        to the throat.

 The first one says "cold"

 and the second says "warm,"

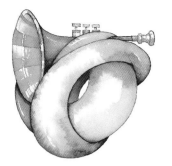

the third plays a tune that would calm any storm.

The fourth is a star

and the fifth is a stone

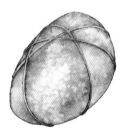

and the sixth is a doll with a coat
like my own.

I went out on Monday to see what I'd see,
And I saw a young giant who was hot as could be.
"The trouble," he said, "with being long in the leg
Is the sun fries my head as though it were an egg."

So I bit off my button (the one that said "cold"),
And I handed it up for his hot hand to hold.

And when he'd cooled down,
he began to emote,

"What a megacooliferous,
marvelous coat!"

I went out on Tuesday to see what I'd see,
And I saw a white swan lying under a tree.
Her feathers were frozen, all smothered in snow,
Though she struggled to fly, her poor wings wouldn't go.
So I bit off my button (the one that said "warm"),

And before long the swan was in fine flying form.
As she took to the air, the first song in her throat
Was, "What a meltificent, marvelous coat!"

I went out on Wednesday to see what I'd see,
And I saw a great ship sailing over the sea.
The rain blew so hard and the wind blew so high,
That the captain and crew began loudly to cry.

So I bit off my button (that played a sweet tune),
And its beautiful song calmed that storm very soon.
Then the captain and crew, as away they did float,
Sang, "Ahoy to that maritime, marvelous coat!"

I went out on Thursday to see what I'd see,
And I saw an old wizard who whispered to me,
"Since I wore out my wand, at my spells I'm a flop —
All I've left is a stick with no magic on top."

So I bit off my button (the one like a star),
And the way that it stuck to that stick was bizarre.

When the wiz waved his wand, in the heavens it wrote,
"What a magical, mystical, marvelous coat!"

I went out on Friday to see what I'd see,
And I saw a snake searching for something for tea.
"I'll sssslip down thissss burrow," he hissed with a grin,
And three frightened bunnies squealed, "Don't let him in!"
So I bit off my button (the one like a stone),
And I rolled it in front of the hole with a groan.

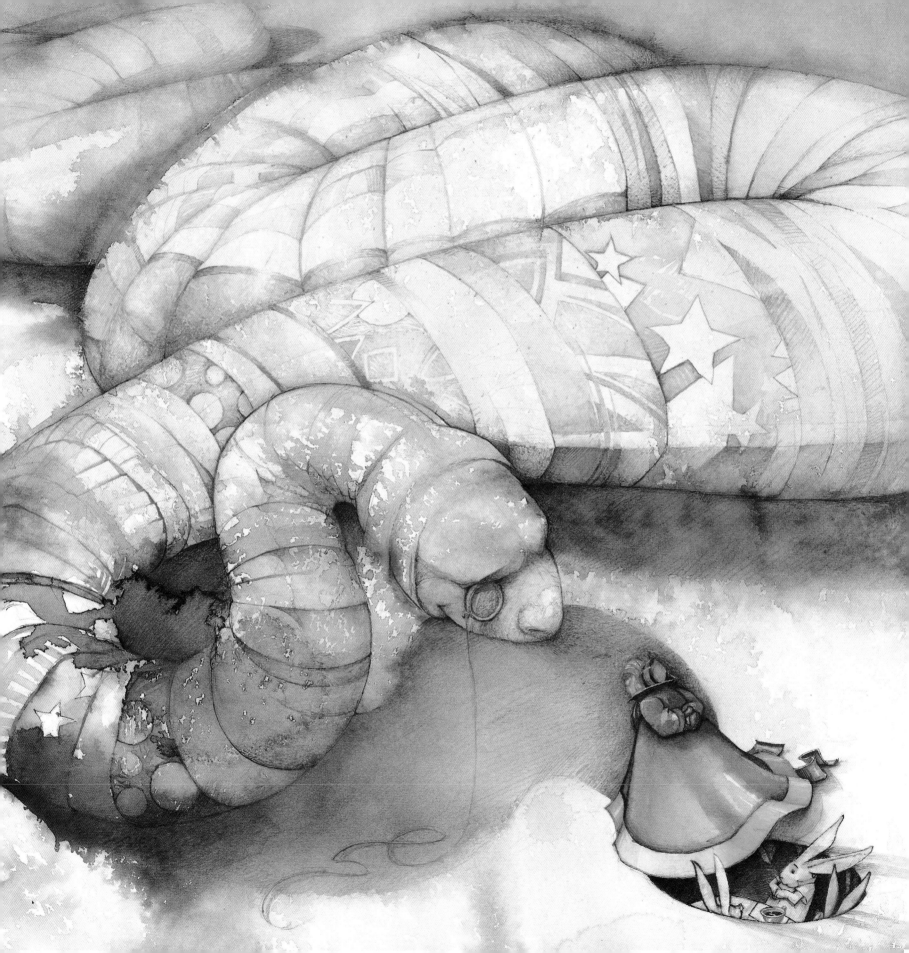

As the snake slithered off, the three bunnies, I quote,
Said, "What a most meal-stopping, marvelous coat!"

I went out on Saturday to see what I'd see,
And I saw a small elf who seemed sad as could be.
"I've searched down below," he sighed, "and up above,
But I can't find a smallish somebody to love."
So I bit off my button (the dolly herself),
And she yawned and she stretched and she smiled at the elf.

As they danced in the twilight, they sang with one note,
"What a matchmaking, marrying, marvelous coat!"

On Sunday my mother and father said, "Child,
To lose all six buttons seems wanton and wild."

Before I could answer, the pockets they tried,
And six magic buttons were waiting inside!
So we sewed back the cold and we sewed back the warm,
And we sewed back the tune that could calm any storm;
We sewed back the star and we sewed back the stone,
And we sewed back the doll with the coat like my own.

As I buttoned my coat, Mother opened the door,
And in came a crowd I'd seen somewhere before:

Some sailors, a giant,
a swan, and an elf,
three rabbits, one wiz,
and my dolly herself!

We kissed in the kitchen,
we hugged in the hall,
and we skipped up the stairs
as we sang one and all,

"It's fashion, it's couture, it's high, and it's haute,
That megacooliferous,
truly meltificent,
meal-stopping,
magical,

maritime,
marrying,

mostly just marvelous coat!"